THE LITTLE
SEA HORSE

Also available in Hodder Storybooks
by Helen Cresswell

A Game of Catch
A Gift from Winklesea
Whatever Happened in Winklesea?
Mystery at Winklesea

THE LITTLE
SEA HORSE

HELEN CRESSWELL

Illustrated by Jason Cockcroft

*Hodder
Children's
Books*

a division of Hodder Headline plc

Text Copyright © 1964 by Helen Rowe
Illustrations Copyright © 1995 by Jason Cockcroft

First published in Great Britain in 1964
by Oliver Boyd Ltd.

This edition first published 1995
by Hodder Children's Books

The right of Helen Rowe to be identified as the Author
of this Work has been asserted by her in accordance with
the Copyright, Designs and Patents Act 1988.

10 9 8 7

ISBN 0 340 63461 8

Typeset by Avon Dataset Ltd, Bidford-on-Avon

Printed and bound in Great Britain by
Cox & Wyman Ltd, Reading, Berkshire

Hodder Children's Books
a division of Hodder Headline plc
338 Euston Road
London NW1 3BH

For my Father
with love and appreciation

Contents

A Surprise from the Sea

Once upon a time a little girl called Molly Flower lived by the shore of a grey sea. Her home was a tubby wooden houseboat that bobbed on the waters of a wide and beautiful bay ringed by mountains. She lived with her father, who was a fisherman. He went to sea in the grey mist of dawn and came again in the thick white mists of evening. Or perhaps he spent the day on the beach mending or painting his boat, and Molly would help him, threading the nets or sewing the tattered sails of his fishing boat, the *Grey Gull*.

When her father was away Molly spent the days on the shore, poking in pools left by the tide, teasing crabs that hid under the black rotting wood of the jetty, and collecting shells. Sometimes she climbed the warm sandy steps that led up to the village of Piskerton and played till evening with the children who lived in the cottages.

Her newest friend was a boy called Peter who had brought a string of donkeys to give rides to the children. He was an orphan and used to looking after himself. On warm nights he slung a hammock between the pillars of the pier, but when it was cold or wet he found shelter with a friendly fisherman.

One night Molly sat dangling her bare feet over the edge of the sea wall and waiting for the first glimpse of brown sails far away on the world's rim. A blue dusk was gathering. Behind her the yellow lamps of the cottages bloomed one by one, and the fisher folk stood on the steps in twos and threes talking softly or crooning songs as old as the sea itself.

The fishing boats came over the rim of the world; trim and sturdy they travelled the grey water. At last they knocked against the sea wall and the men leaped ashore, throwing ropes and heaving and splashing and shouting to one another. Their shadows were huge and swaying in the lantern light, they seemed like giants, and they laughed and sang until the whole village sprang to life in the darkness.

The villagers crowded round to stare at the catch of fish. They lay in piles of silver on the cold quayside, plump and shining like ripe fruit. When everyone had admired the day's catch they drifted away to their homes, the men hungry and ready for their hot stew and a blazing fire.

That night Molly could see no sign of her father. She had seen his fishing boat, the *Grey Gull*, coming in with the fleet, but she had not seen him among the other fishermen, and now she was left all alone on the dark quayside.

She strained her eyes in the darkness, but all she could see was masts pointing skywards and the faint glow from the heaps of fish. She listened, but heard only the wet licking of waves on the sea wall and the clatter of feet on cobbled streets in the distance.

She shivered and drew the woollen shawl more closely round her shoulders.

"Perhaps he did not see me and has gone back to the *Tubby Boat*," she thought. "If I go home perhaps I shall find him there already."

She was turning away when she heard her father's voice but could not tell where it was coming from.

"Father!" she called. "Where are you?"

"I'm down here, in the boat. Can you give me a hand?"

She ran to where her father's boat was moored to a ring in the sea wall and leaned over.

"Father, why are you still in the boat? I thought you had gone home."

"I waited until everyone had gone home because I did not want a lot of noise and excitement. I have found something today, Molly, so strange and wonderful that I hardly know what it is myself."

"What is it? What is it?" asked Molly excitedly, leaning over so far that she almost lost her balance.

"I shall be fishing you out if you don't stand still," said Mr Flower, laughing. "See, I'll pass it up to you. It is not very heavy, but hold it gently until I come."

He stretched up his arms, and Molly reached down and felt something very soft and warm. She looked down but could not see what it was, only that it was white and was shining faintly even in the darkness. She stood alone on the windy quay prickling with excitement.

Her father clambered up beside her.

"Well?" he said. "What do you make of that?"

"What is it, Father?" asked Molly. "Do tell me. And where did you find it?"

"Wait until we are home," he said.

He gently lifted the animal from Molly's arms and taking her by the hand, strode off towards the other end of the bay. In the *Tubby Boat* there was a hot, hungry smell of stew, the light from the fire stroked the walls, and the shadows yawned and stretched like sleepy cats. Molly's father laid the animal on the patchwork rug before the fire. Molly knelt beside it, staring in wonder.

It was a tiny horse of purest white, so delicate that he seemed to be carved from ice. His hooves were of gold and they shone yellow in the firelight, and his ears pricked like petals, as though he were listening. His eyes were as clear and yellow as September moons.

"Father," whispered Molly, "isn't he beautiful? Where did you find him?"

"I drew him in with my nets. When I saw him lying there at the bottom of the boat I thought I was dreaming. I would have put him back in the sea but he seemed tired. His eyes were closed and he hardly seemed to breathe. When he has been fed and rested I shall be able to take him back next time the boats go out."

"Oh, Father, can't we keep him? See how tiny and white he is! How can he live in the rough seas? Please let me keep him here!"

Her father laughed and shook his head.

"There are tinier creatures in the sea than this," he said. "I don't think he would be happy if we kept him here. But fetch him some milk, perhaps he is hungry."

So Molly fetched a saucer of milk and the tiny horse began to drink. Then he struggled to his feet, wobbling a little on his long thin legs, and his moon-yellow eyes moving curiously and unwinkingly round the cabin. He took a few unsteady steps and then sank down again in front of the fire, his eyes drooping.

"He's tired still," said Molly's father. "Come away and let him sleep. It's past your bedtime, too."

"But say I can keep the little sea horse," begged Molly.

Her father smiled and shook his head again.

"I'm not making any promises," he said.

And so Molly went to bed. But she lay awake for a long time on her bunk staring at the stars in the porthole and thinking of the white sea horse with his hooves of beaten gold.

Mr Winkle Steps In

Next morning the sea horse was as lively as a cricket. He twirled round the cabin on his spindly legs, and his dandelion-puff mane spun round his head in a halo hiding his yellow eyes.

"He's lively enough to go back into the sea straight away," said Mr Flower.

"Oh, please let me keep him just for one day," begged Molly. "I want to show him to Peter."

"Very well," agreed her father. "Just for one day. But tomorrow I shall take him and put him back in the sea where he belongs."

That day her father went with the other fishermen to a fishing town farther along the coast to buy new nets and tackle ready for the winter.

When he had gone Molly plaited a rope from seaweed and made it into a collar and lead. The sea horse stood quietly while she put it on and they jumped from the rockety *Tubby Boat* and set off for the village.

The sea horse kept tugging so that he could walk right at the very edge of the sea, picking his way delicately over the smooth bleached pebbles, and dipping his buttercup hooves in the grey water as often as he could. The seagulls screeched with surprise, crabs poked their heads from under stones to stare, and even the waves seemed startled, their white crests of hair sticking up on end.

Soon they were under the pier where the air was very green and cold and a strong, wet smell of fish and seaweed came up from the sand. There was no sign of Peter, though in the distance Molly could see the donkeys racing on the level sands. Urchin and Rascal were in the lead as usual.

Molly cupped her hands and called: "Peter!"

A hollow echo ran between the arches and whispered right down to the very edge of the sea: "Peter, Peter, Peter . . ."

She waited, and then she heard the reply: "I'm here!"

"Here, here, here . . ." the echoes sighed.

She ran weaving through the pillars up the beach and saw Peter's tousled head sticking over the side of his hammock high among the beams and rafters of the pier.

"Hello! Don't shout so loudly! I might have fallen out!"

"Get up, lazy!" said Molly. "Why are you still in your hammock?"

"I didn't go to bed until midnight. The tide was in and I had to wait until it went out before I could climb up."

"Come down quickly, Peter, I want to show you something."

"Here I come."

He swung himself over the side of the hammock

and clambered down the beams and pillars until he sprang nimbly to Molly's side. His eyes grew huge when he saw the sea horse.

"My goodness! Whatever's that? That's not a donkey!"

"Of course not. It's a sea horse. My father caught it in his nets last night."

"A sea horse!" Peter shouted and jumped high into the air. "A real live sea horse! Don't you know what that means? Luck! It's lucky to find a sea horse. It's lucky even to touch one. Quick, let me touch him!"

He grabbed at the little horse, who shied away in alarm, but he managed to touch its flyaway mane with the very tips of his fingers.

"Hurray!" he shouted gleefully. "I touched the lucky sea horse!"

Then he turned and began running up the beach, shouting at the top of his voice: "Molly's got a sea horse! Molly's got a lucky sea horse!"

"Stop, Peter, stop!" she called.

But the wind blew her voice sideways and away

out over the sea and Peter ran on, growing smaller and smaller in the distance. She could see him running up the steps to the village and his voice was blown back to her, still shouting: "Molly's got a sea horse! Come and touch the lucky sea horse!"

Molly gave up and stood for a few minutes panting.

"Oh dear," she said. "Now I suppose the whole village will want to see him."

She began to walk back with the sea horse towards the *Tubby Boat* across the bay. When they reached home they went down to the cabin, and Molly gave the horse a saucer of milk. As he was lapping it up she heard the sound of voices coming nearer, and she thought she heard her name being called. She went up on to the deck, and an amazing sight met her eyes.

Every single person in the village seemed to be there, crowding on the shingle and peering and craning his neck to catch a glimpse of the sea horse. At the very front was the village Mayor, Mr Winkle, who had put on his red robe and gold chain but had bare feet and rolled-up trousers because he had been shrimping in the pools when Peter had brought the news. At his side stood Mr Bellow, the village Crier, with his big brass bell and three-cornered hat.

25

When the villagers saw Molly standing on the deck of the *Tubby Boat* they all stopped talking, and for a moment it was so quiet that you could hear the water lapping on the sides of the boat. Everyone nudged everyone else, hoping that someone would pluck up courage to say the first word.

Molly stood waiting. She caught sight of Peter hiding right at the back and looking rather red and ashamed of himself. At last, Mr Winkle spoke.

"It has come to my notice," he said, "that you have a – er – er – sea horse in your possession."

"Yes, I have," Molly told him. "But I brought him here because I don't want him to be frightened. If you want to see him you must come in ones and twos and not make so much noise."

Mr Winkle cleared his throat.

"Mr Bellow, read the notice," he commanded.

Mr Bellow then cleared *his* throat, took a deep breath and rang his bell noisily, shouting very loudly at the same time.

"Oyez! Oyez! It is hereby proclaimed by order

of His Worship the Mayor that the white sea horse found in Piskerton Bay should be handed over to the Mayor, to be kept safely as the village mascot and to bring luck and good fortune to the people of Piskerton. Oyez! Oyez! Oyez!"

Someone in the crowd gave a feeble cheer and began to clap, and the next minute all the people were clapping and cheering and shouting.

"The sea horse! We want to see it! Bring out the sea horse!"

At that very moment the tiny white horse stepped up on to the deck of the *Tubby Boat* beside Molly and a little gasp of wonder ran through the crowd as they saw him standing there, his golden hooves flashing fire in the sunlight.

"Ah!" they breathed. "Look! Isn't he beautiful?"

Then, before anyone could stop him, a little ragged boy in the crowd jumped forward and grabbed the lead of plaited seaweed and tugged the little horse away from Molly. She tried to stop him but it was too late.

The crowd of fisher folk flocked round him,

admiring him and trying to touch his soft white coat. Soon they marched away in procession, led by Mr Winkle proudly holding the plaited seaweed, and leaving Molly all alone on the deck of the *Tubby Boat*.

The Bamboo Cage

When Molly's father came home that night and found that the sea horse had been taken away he was very angry.

"We shall see about that!" he said.

And as soon as he had eaten his stew and changed into his best suit he went marching up to the village to see the Mayor.

When he reached the Mayor's house he rapped sharply on the brass knocker and waited, but there was no reply. The parrot which swung in a cage in the gusty porch shrieked: "The Mayor's gone to the village hall!"

So off Mr Flower went up the narrow cobbled streets in search of him.

There was a crowd of people standing under the lamplight outside the village hall and they all seemed to be staring at something. Mr Flower pushed his way forward and saw there on the steps, his yellow eyes wide with terror, the little white sea horse.

Someone had made a cage for him of woven bamboo, and lying in front of it were little gifts of flowers and painted shells from people who hoped that the sea horse would bring them luck. The cage was not very big, so that anyone who wished could reach through the bars and touch him.

"How dare you!" boomed Mr Flower, in a deep angry voice.

Everyone turned in surprise to see who had spoken. He stood on the steps of the village hall and faced the crowd below him.

"How dare you come and take my sea horse and put him in a cage!" he said. "And don't you see how cruel you are being? Look how frightened he is. You ought to be ashamed of yourselves!"

The people, who were really very kind at heart, hung their heads and shuffled their feet, and some of them began to murmur: "Let the poor thing go. It's a shame!"

"No!" thundered another voice, even louder than Mr Flower's. It was the Mayor, who had come out of the village hall and was standing on the top of the steps frowning sternly.

"No!" repeated Mr Winkle, digging his thumbs deeply into his waistcoat pockets. "I say that animal shall stay here."

"I beg your pardon," said Mr Flower politely,

because after all Mr Winkle was the Mayor. "I didn't know you were there."

"Well, I am here," said the Mayor. "And as Mayor of Piskerton I am the one to decide whether or not to keep the sea horse. And my mind is made up. He shall stay."

There was a short silence.

"Stay – he – shall," repeated the Mayor, with a long, terrible pause between each word.

Mr Flower climbed a step higher so that he could look the Mayor in the eye.

"Why?" he asked.

A little gasp ran through the crowd. Here was excitement! Mr Flower of the *Tubby Boat* arguing with the Mayor himself in front of the whole village. They pressed closer eagerly.

"Why?" repeated Mr Winkle. "I'll tell you why. Because that sea horse means good luck, that's why."

He turned to the crowd.

"Is there anyone here who doesn't want good luck?" he asked.

"No!" they all roared in delight.

Mr Flower stood his ground.

"I want good luck as much as anyone," he said, "but I don't think it's right to keep that poor little creature shut up in a cage on the steps of the village hall. I would like to make a suggestion."

"You may do so," said Mr Winkle graciously. "I don't mind hearing other people's opinions as long as it is quite clearly understood that what *I* say is what goes."

"I suggest that the whole village should line up and one by one they could go by the cage and touch the sea horse. Then everyone will have good luck and we can let him go."

Some of the people in the crowd called out "Good idea!" and "Yes, let him go!" and Mr Winkle frowned.

"Well?" said Mr Flower, "what do you say, Mr Mayor?"

"I say this," said Mr Winkle. "I say that your idea is a good one, as far as it goes. As far as it goes. But there's another reason why I say that the sea horse should stay here. As you all know, in two weeks' time Piskerton will be holding a great fair and festival. And the King and Queen are coming to open it.

"Think," said Mr Winkle, his cheeks growing pink with excitement at the thought, "think of the honour it would be to be able to say to Their Majesties:'The people of Piskerton have captured a real live sea horse, and . . .' " here Mr Winkle paused dramatically, " '. . . and they wish to present it to Your Majesties as a humble token of their loyalty and affection.' "

"Hurrah!" shouted a little boy in the crowd.

"Hurrah! Bravo!" shouted everyone else.

"Go home, Mr Flower," shouted the same little boy and then ducked behind a lamp-post, hoping he would be out of sight.

"What have you to say to that, Mr Flower?" enquired the Mayor grandly.

"It certainly would be a great honour," agreed Mr Flower slowly. "But I still don't like the idea of keeping the horse here in a cage. It isn't right."

"Very well," said Mr Winkle, who was in a good mood now that the crowd was on his side. "We will build a high fence round the village green so that he can play on the grass. He will also be able to swim in the duck pond if he wishes. If he doesn't like ducks, then the ducks shall be moved. We will put seaweed in the pond to make it seem more like home. He shall have every comfort. I personally will inspect the village green every day to see that everything is to his liking. What do you say to that?"

"That is a very handsome offer, Your Worship," said Mr Flower, "and I agree to it. Mind, I don't say that I don't think the horse wouldn't be happier back in the sea, but if we are to make him a gift to Their Majesties then it's the best that can be done."

"Then the matter is settled," said the Major. "I will have the fence built tomorrow."

When they saw that the excitement was over the people began to clatter off down the windy streets to their homes and soon the square was deserted. The lamplighter came plodding by and snuffed out the lamp and all was quiet.

But the white sea horse in his bamboo cage stood for a long time in the starlight, straining his petal ears for the faint sound of the sea washing the pebbles and of seagulls crying in their sleep.

A Topsy-Turvy Market

As the Mayor had promised, workmen came the very next day to put up a fence round the village green, and by evening the sea horse was in his new home. He stamped his golden hooves on the soft turf and whirled in and out of the pond in a halo of spray and everyone agreed that he looked very much happier.

The Mayor came to inspect him and declared that he looked very well and comfortable. He went so far as to say that on the whole he was probably better off than he had been in the sea, for there are no sharks in duck ponds.

In the evening Molly and Peter went to see him. He looked more strange and beautiful than ever against the green grass in the glow of the setting sun that turned his hooves to fire. He ran lightly to the fence when he saw Molly and his yellow eyes lit up. He stood for a few seconds while she stroked him and then he was off again, skimming over the grass in a fine mist of dew, never still, prancing and rearing and tossing his tiny head.

The next day was market day, when the people from the neighbouring countryside came into Piskerton to buy and sell and enjoy a day by the sea.

"There will be plenty of children who want rides on the donkeys," said Peter. "Meet me under the pier at seven o'clock in the morning."

But the first thing Molly heard when she woke the next morning was the rain beating steadily on the deck and pattering on the porthole as it slanted in from the sea. She looked out and saw that the sea was a dull grey and a little cold wind blew it up in ruffles.

By nine o'clock it still had not stopped raining so Molly put on her yellow oilskins and sou'wester and plodded through the wet sand to the village.

She found Peter in the stables where the donkeys were kept, polishing their harnesses. He was not in a very good mood, and the donkeys themselves seemed restless and fidgety. They kept snorting and tossing their heads impatiently, wanting to be out in the open and racing down the sands instead of cooped in the warm, steamy stable with the rain beating on the roof.

"Let's go to the market," said Peter. "Perhaps the rain will clear this afternoon."

So they left the dim stables, and with the wind tugging at their oilskins they climbed the cobbled street, with its blue puddles, to the square in front of the village hall. The market was so noisy and crowded and full of colour that it was easy to forget the rain and grey skies. The stalls bulged with good things, from blue-shelled mussels to ballooning vegetable marrows, from cockles in vinegar to cornflowers from cottage gardens.

Peter and Molly climbed to the top step of the village hall and looked down on the bustling scene. In the distance they could see the village green and the tiny white speck that was the sea horse.

They saw something else, too, that made them blink with surprise.

Standing in a string peering over the top of the fence round the green were the donkeys.

As Molly and Peter watched, they suddenly turned and started galloping up the main street to the village square.

"I must have left the stable door open!" gasped Peter. "Quickly, Molly, we must stop them!"

But it was too late. The next minute the donkeys, with Urchin leading them, charged into the square. There was a tremendous crash and jangle as they knocked over a stall and left its owner with a saucepan over his head and his pots and pans rolling merrily over the cobbles.

People screamed, children laughed and grabbed the oranges and apples that went skittling over the pavements, and the donkeys brayed gleefully. Mr Bellow sat in the gutter with a string of onions round his neck, ringing his brass bell and shouting something.

Mr Winkle came storming up the street, clutching his hat with one hand and waving a stick in the other.

"Who's chewed the heads off all the flowers in my garden?" he yelled. "Who's eaten all my prize Michaelmas daisies?"

The donkeys gathered themselves into a little knot and plunged down the street toward him. Urchin snatched off his hat as they galloped past and the next minute they had gone, leaving the market in ruins.

Mr Winkle stamped through the square and everyone stood aside in silence to let him pass. They could see that he was very angry. Just as he reached the bottom of the steps he slipped on a broken egg and sat promptly on the pavement. The people tittered and then tried to turn their titters into coughs, and Mr Winkle got up with as much dignity as possible. His face was like thunder.

"This is the most outrageous thing I have ever seen in my whole life," he said. "Those donkeys have deliberately chewed the heads off every single flower in my garden. They have stolen my hat and ruined the market . . . My mind is made up. The donkeys must go. By seven o'clock tomorrow morning there must not be a single donkey left in Piskerton, or-or—"

He choked hard and tried to think of something to say.

"Or else!" he said at last.

Then he turned and marched past Molly and Peter into the village hall.

"We had better go and find the donkeys," whispered Peter, "before they do any more damage."

They pushed their way through the tangle of fallen stalls and excited people, and as they went they could hear people saying to one another: "If this is the kind of good luck the sea horse has brought us we'd be better off if we let him go."

Out at sea the Mayor's hat bobbed on the waves with several delighted seagulls perched on its brim. But that was something Mr Winkle would never know.

The Old Man of the Lighthouse

The next day the donkeys had gone, just as the Mayor had ordered. But the strange thing was, no one knew where they had gone. The villagers could talk of nothing else. The marks of the donkeys' hooves went right down the beach to the very edge of the sea, and then stopped! It was as if they had walked right into the very heart of the sea.

A meeting was held, and it was decided that Molly and Peter should row out and see the Old Man of the Lighthouse. He was the only person who might be able to solve the mystery.

The Old Man of the Lighthouse was very old and wise, and he had lived alone on the lighthouse rock for so long that he belonged to the sea as much as to the land. He understood the sea as if it were the palm of his own hand. Some people said that he went under the sea itself and knew all its secrets. If the donkeys had been stolen by the sea, then he would know.

The whole village trooped down to the harbour to see Molly and Peter off. A fisherman lent them his yellow-painted rowing boat, for the rest of the fleet was out at sea that day. In the far distance they could see the lighthouse pointing like a warning finger into the restless sky. A strong wind was blowing from the sea, and the waves were greeny-grey and choppy. The seagulls flocked together.

Willing hands carried the dinghy down to the water's edge, and Molly and Peter climbed in.

"Good-bye, Molly. Good-bye, Peter," cried the villagers. "Come back safely!"

Molly and Peter took the oars and began to

row until the villagers were only tiny specks on the horizon.

Seagulls whirled in circles on the wind in their wake, screaming uneasily. Once they were out of the shelter of the bay the sea became rougher and the wind fresher, whipping up the waves in green ringlets and blowing the salt spray on to their faces. All the time the pointing finger of the lighthouse loomed up larger. Soon they could see the white surf simmering round the sharp rocks on which the lighthouse stood.

"Look!" shouted Peter into the wind. "Isn't that someone moving, out there on the rocks?"

"Yes," shouted Molly, tasting the spray salt on her lips. "That's the Old Man himself."

In a few minutes the lighthouse was towering above them, and Molly threw a rope over one of the iron stakes driven into the wall and pulled the boat in. A flight of rocky steps led up to the lighthouse and they clambered up them, thinking how icy cold they were from the endless washing by the sea.

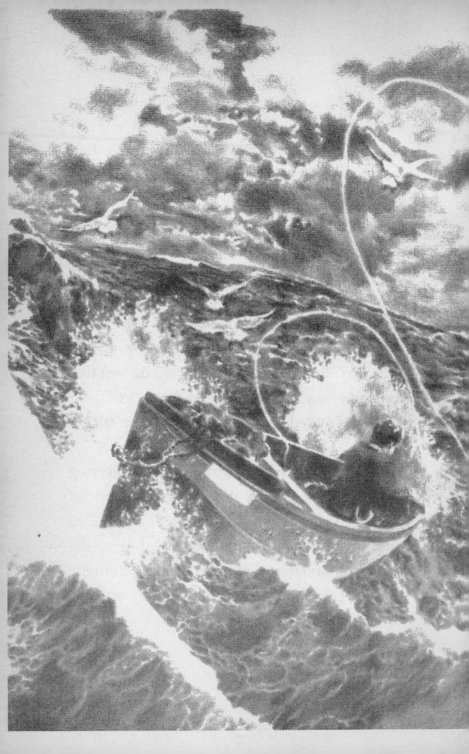

At the top of the steps stood the Old Man of the Lighthouse to greet them.

His long grey hair and beard floated on the wind and his grey eyes glittered. A thousand suns had beaten his skin to copper and his eyes were very strange. He had gazed so long into the measureless distances of stars and seas that when he looked at Peter and Molly his eyes seemed to be focussed always on something beyond them, like those of a blind man. But his smile was kind.

"Good day," he said. "You have travelled a long way to see me. Have you come for my help?"

"Oh yes, please!" said Molly. "We have come about Peter's donkeys. We think they have been taken away by the sea."

The Old Man of the Lighthouse nodded his head slowly, looking from one to the other.

"Come inside," he said.

He turned and led the way up the rock to the lighthouse. Hundreds of seagulls were perched on the rocks so thickly that they looked like patches of melting snow. There were other birds, too, with strange curved beaks and mottled plumages of greys and browns. Their cries were blown together by the wind into a kind of harsh music.

Once inside the lighthouse it was suddenly quiet and dim. The sea boomed beneath them with a distant roar. The furniture was very simple and was made of wood, and the walls were lined with shelves of books, ships in bottles, and rare shells.

A flight of stone steps spiralled up to the lamp room, and in the floor was a trap door with a huge iron ring.

"Tell me now about the donkeys," said the Old Man.

So Molly told him the whole story, ending with how they had found the footmarks disappearing at the edge of the sea.

"We thought perhaps they had been stolen by the sea as punishment for keeping the white sea horse prisoner," she said.

The Old Man nodded.

"That is what has happened," he told her. "But don't be alarmed. The donkeys are safe and happy and will not be harmed."

"But I want them back!" cried Peter. "I don't want my donkeys to stay at the bottom of the sea. How can I get them back?"

"There is only one way," replied the Old Man of the Lighthouse, rising and going over to a cupboard.

"What is it?" asked Peter.

"Have patience," said the Old Man. "You will see, you will see."

He took three glasses from the cupboard and a flask of golden liquid and measured it out carefully. He gave a glass each to Molly and Peter and kept one for himself.

"Drink it," he commanded.

So Molly and Peter sipped the golden liquid. They found it sweet and pleasant to taste, and they drank the rest of it down greedily.

"Good," said the Old Man when the glasses were empty. "Now come with me."

He went over to the trap door and pulled hard at the enormous iron ring. With a groan it swung open, revealing a flight of rocky steps. The Old Man lit a storm lantern and beckoned to the children to follow him.

They began to descend the steep rock steps. Their shadows swayed on the wet rock of the walls and the air was icy. Echoes shuttled back and forth around them, and all the while the boom of the sea grew louder until at last they were almost deafened by it.

The Old Man stopped, and they saw that they had reached the bottom and that a narrow creek ran at their feet. They could make out the outline of a boat. In the distance they could see the faint glow of daylight.

Wordlessly the Old Man got in and the children followed. With strong steady strokes he rowed the boat toward the opening and suddenly they were out of the cave and on the open sea, almost blinded by the brilliant sunlight.

The Enchanted Donkeys

They went through the collar of surf that encircled the lighthouse rocks into the calmer water beyond. The wind had dropped and the sun was shining and the sea was a smooth glassy green. Molly felt very strange and far away, almost lulled to sleep by the steady rhythm of the oars, and she thought drowsily that it must be something to do with the golden liquid they had drunk.

"Why did we drink it, I wonder?" she thought. "And why has he brought us here?"

The Old Man stopped rowing and drew in the oars. He fixed his faraway eyes on Molly and Peter.

"Look down into the sea," he said.

Dreamily Molly turned her head and looked over the side. Her gaze went down and down, right through the clear swaying depths to the very floor of the ocean. At her side she heard Peter gasp with delight and wonder.

The fish sailed by smoothly and slowly winding their quiet ways, barely stirring the seaweed as they passed. The sand of the sea bed was white and fine and scattered with a thousand wonders, so that Molly hardly knew where to look first. She stared at the drifting shells and quicksilver shoals and groping sponges, and she did not even notice that the Old Man of the Lighthouse had picked up the oars and was rowing again.

The sea unrolled before them like a green carpet, and time stood still. It seemed a hundred years before Molly heard Peter's voice, sounding a long way off as if he were at the bottom of a deep well, crying: "Look! Look! There they are!"

The six donkeys lay fast asleep on the sea bed, their wild ears lying as flat and quiet as if they had been ironed down. Not a stir did they make,

not a twitch of the nose, not a flick of the tail.
Never had any donkeys been so still, and certainly
never these donkeys.

"Urchin, wake up!" shouted Peter, leaning far out over the side of the boat. "Rascal! Urchin! Wake up!"

But the dreaming donkeys made not the least stir. The spell of the sea was on them.

"You will never wake them by calling," said the Old Man of the Lighthouse. "Their sleep is too deep. They are enchanted."

"Then how can I wake them up?" cried Peter in desperation.

"Only the white sea horse can do that," replied the Old Man. "So now you know what is to be done."

"But the Mayor will never let him go!" cried Molly. "He is going to give him to the King and Queen at the festival."

"We must steal him away," said Peter. "I don't care for a thousand Mayors. Quickly, Molly, let us go back to the shore."

Molly took a last look at the sleeping donkeys, like great furry mats on the ocean floor, and the boat sped smoothly away.

Still Molly gazed over the side, watching the strange life fathoms below, but gradually she found it more and more difficult to make out the white sand of the ocean bed. The water that earlier had become as clear as glass began to mist over again, and now the fish were no more than shadowy shapes. Then at last all she could see was the surface of the water, calm and blue and deckled with little lines of foam. The golden wine they had drunk had lost its power.

As soon as they reached the lighthouse the Old Man led the way on to the rock where their own boat was moored. It was very hot now. The sun blazed down and there was not a breath of wind. He gazed up into the sky with his faraway eyes.

"There will be a storm," he said. "Goodbye, and good luck!"

They promised him that if they were successful in setting the sea horse free, they would send up a rocket to tell him the news. Then they scrambled back into the boat and pushed off. They rowed as hard as they could back to shore.

63

A great cheer went up as they drew the boat up on to the shingle and climbed out. Everyone crowded round them asking questions.

"What did the Old Man of the Lighthouse tell you?"

"Have you found out where the donkeys are?"

Peter held up his hand for silence and immediately everyone stopped talking.

"We have found out where the donkeys are," he said. "We saw them with our own eyes, asleep on the floor of the ocean. They have been enchanted, and the Old Man of the Lighthouse says that the only way we can set them free is to release the white sea horse. As you know, Mr Winkle is going to give the sea horse to the King and Queen tomorrow at the festival, so if we are going to set him free it must be done now!"

"Hurrah!" shouted the crowd. "Set him free. Let's go and set him free."

"Wait!" boomed a voice from the quayside, and turning round they saw Mr Winkle standing there.

"That sea horse belongs to the whole village," said Mr Winkle. "If anything is to be done the whole village must have a say in it. Nothing is to be done until the fishing fleet comes in."

The crowd all muttered, and some of them said: "He thinks there will be a storm and they won't get here in time." But the fisherman who had lent his boat to Peter and Molly, and who could read the weather like a book, said: "We agree, Your Worship. There is no harm in waiting until tonight when the boats come in."

Mr Winkle gave a triumphant smile and turned away, and the crowd began to break up.

"I wonder why Mr Winkle looked so pleased with himself," said Peter slowly. "Do you think he is going to play a trick on us?"

"I think that he suspects there is going to be a storm and is hoping that the fleet will put into another harbour to shelter and not come home tonight. Then tomorrow it will be too late," said Molly.

"It won't," said Peter doggedly. "Because if the fleet is not home by nightfall, I shall go tonight and set the sea horse free myself!"

The Storm

That night the village was in a fever of excitement. There were all the preparations for the festival tomorrow to be completed, and then there was the suspense of waiting for the fleet to come in so that the sea horse could be set free. The people knew that if the storm broke before the fleet came in all would be lost.

A small boy was posted on the sea wall with a telescope and told to shout loudly as soon as he could sight sails on the horizon.

Mr Winkle walked round the village in his fine robes, making sure that all the preparations were properly completed, and all the time wearing that secret little smile.

As it began to grow dusk the huge black clouds rolled up in the distance, and the air grew very still and quiet. Now that all the work was done the fisher people gathered in groups on the shingle to wait. They talked in low excited whispers, rather frightened by the breathless silence.

The seagulls were flying very low and uttering uneasy cries, and a strange yellow light flooded the harbour. Every moment the sky darkened

and still there was no sign of the fleet. Then a shout shattered the silence.

"I see them! I see them!" yelled the small boy with the telescope. He danced on the sea wall in his excitement. His mother made him get down, and they all strained their eyes for the first glimpse of sails. Slowly their shadowy shapes could be seen far out on the bay, and at that moment there came the first distant rumble of thunder.

"Mr Winkle does not look so happy now," whispered Molly. Sure enough, the Mayor's face was as black as the sky itself. He began picking up stones and hurling them out as far as he could into the sea, and the people smiled and nudged one another. They enjoyed outwitting their own Mayor.

As the boats came nearer, the voices of the fishermen singing floated over the waves, and when at last the boats scrunched on the shingle everyone crowded round the men, all trying at the same time to explain what had happened.

Molly ran to her father and told him quickly all that had happened that day. He listened hard, and when she had finished he went and stood on the sea wall and called for silence. By now it was completely dark and they could only see his outline against the sky.

"People of Piskerton, do you wish to obey the voice of the Old Man of the Lighthouse?" he asked in a ringing voice.

"We do!" shouted the crowd.

"Good. I wanted the sea horse to be set free right from the very beginning," he said. "But I'm not the man to say 'I told you so.' We can all make mistakes. So what do you say we shake hands and be friends, Mr Winkle?"

The crowd cheered, and Mr Winkle could do nothing else but go slowly forward and shake Mr Flower by the hand.

"And now," cried Mr Flower, "it's off to the village green!"

Everyone began to surge forward, but Mr Winkle stood at the top of the steps and spread out his arms to stop them. He was determined that he was going to give some orders for a change.

"Stand back," he said. "There is no need for everyone in the village to go rushing up to the green. I will go and fetch the sea horse while you stay here."

"I don't trust him," whispered Peter, and stepping forward he said politely:"Don't you think it would be better, Your Worship, if Molly went? After all, it is her sea horse and he's used to her. He might be afraid of someone as grand as you."

"Yes, let Molly go!" roared the crowd, who also suspected Mr Winkle of mischief.

"I'll get the rocket ready to fire while you're gone," whispered Peter.

Molly climbed the stone steps and set off alone

up the dark, cobbled streets. As she went the first
heavy drops of rain began to fall, and there was a
flash of lightning.

"Ah!" gasped the crowd on the beach, watching
the lightning flicker over the sea. "What a storm
there's going to be!"

Molly hurried her steps until she came to the village green. Softly she unlocked the gate and stepped inside.

At that moment a great flash of lightning lit up the whole sky and she saw the white sea horse standing before her, his red-gold hooves and yellow eyes changed to purest silver, and his coat so dazzling that it seemed to throw off a strange luminous glow of its own. He trotted towards her on his spindle legs, and she felt his nose nuzzling in the palm of her hand.

There was no need for the seaweed rope this time. Without a word she began to run back down the street, the rain slanting in her face and the sea horse galloping lightly at her side.

When they reached the harbour front she could see the crowd on the beach waiting for her, their pale faces and yellow oilskins gleaming in the darkness.

"Where's the horse!" they cried. "We can't see him!"

As if in answer the lightning flashed and for a few seconds they saw the tiny horse poised on the sea wall, his hooves and eyes burning silver in the bluish light and his neck stretched eagerly as he sniffed again the salt of the sea. Then they were plunged into darkness again, and Molly heard a soft crunch as the little horse leaped down on to the shingle and raced toward the sea. Again and again the lightning flashed, and as the horse reached the sea's edge the waves seemed to yawn open and swallow him, and he was gone!

Almost in the same instant Peter lit the rocket,

and with a great roar it swept up into the sky and burst into a shower of orange arrows.

The sparks melted into the darkness and for a moment all was quiet. There was a lull in the storm and far out at the rim of the world the lamp of the lighthouse flashed.

Quietly the people turned and began to drift off to their homes, still seeing the little sea horse as he had stood poised on the sea wall with his eyes of silver and his straining neck.

The Spell Breaks

The day of the festival dawned. The sea was calm, the sky was a cloudless blue, and everything was washed and rinsed fresh and shining by the rain of the night before.

By dawn the whole village was astir, the women scrubbing their doorsteps and preparing food, the men decorating their boats with flags and banners in honour of the King and Queen. The Mayor wandered about in a dream, rehearsing his speech to Their Majesties under his breath.

Mr Flower and Molly scrubbed the decks of the *Tubby Boat,* polished the brass fittings and hung her with buntings, and then slowly floated down the bay to the village to take part in the parade of boats.

As they tied up, Molly saw Peter waving to her from the quayside and she ran to meet him.

"Where are the donkeys?" she cried. "Are they in the stables?'

"They haven't come back yet," said Peter.

"Oh, Molly, do you think they ever will?"

"Of course," said Molly stoutly. "The Old Man of the Lighthouse promised. They'll come back, you'll see."

"But I want them back today," said Peter. "All the children will want donkey rides today."

"And what am I going to tell the King and Queen, that is what I should like to know," interrupted a loud voice. It was Mr Winkle. "I told them in my last letter that we had a surprise for them. Now I shall have to explain to them that after all we can't present them with a real live sea horse. But how can I tell them we had to let him go to save the donkeys, when there aren't any donkeys to show? I'm in a very difficult position because of those donkeys of yours."

"Perhaps the donkeys will have come back by

the time the royal procession starts," suggested Molly, who could not help feeling a little sorry for the flustered Mr Winkle.

He snorted.

"Oh no, they won't," he said. "I wish I hadn't let the sea horse go. Fine gratitude he's shown for being set free. If I ever catch another sea horse I shall never let it go. Never!"

He stumped off to his house to give his parrot a last test on the poem he was to say.

The village band had begun to gather on the quay. Their brass instruments glittered in the sun, and their faces were red with scrubbing. The last touches were put to the platform where the King and Queen were to sit, overlooking the bay with its flock of gaily colored boats. Even the seagulls looked whiter than usual.

At last all was ready and the royal coach was due to arrive. As it came rolling over the stone bridge into the village, drawn by four white horses, everyone began to cheer and shout and wave until the whole bay echoed.

Mr Winkle stepped proudly forward and greeted Their Majesties, and when he sat on the platform next to the Queen herself his face was in great danger of splitting with the enormous smile of pride it wore. He made a speech welcoming them to Piskerton and then the King made a speech saying how glad they were to be there and how beautiful the boats in the harbour looked. Then he said how much he and the Queen were looking forward to the "very great surprise" which the Mayor had mentioned in his last letter.

At this the Mayor's face went crimson and the people held their breaths. Poor Mr Winkle!

Bravely he rose to his feet and began to tell the King how Mr Flower had caught a sea horse, and how he, Mr Winkle, had thought what a good idea it would be to present it to Their Majesties on the day of the festival.

"We thought it would bring you luck," he said miserably.

"How wonderful!" cried the Queen, clapping her hands. "A real live sea horse! I have never

seen one before. Where is it?"

"Back in the sea," said Mr Winkle, taking a deep breath.

Then he told the rest of the story, and he was just finishing when suddenly someone shouted: "Look! Look!"

Everyone whirled round and looked down toward the sea, and an astonishing sight met their eyes.

Coming up the beach toward them was the strangest procession they had ever seen, and at its head, miraculously, was the tiny white sea horse himself! His white coat shone in the sun, his hooves glittered red–gold and his eyes were clear and yellow as September moons. Proudly and

delicately he stepped up the stony beach while everyone watched in awestruck silence.

Behind him, in a neat file, were the six donkeys. Their wild ears flapped and their tails twitched. Round their necks they all wore rows and rows of shells, which clashed and jingled as they kept shaking the water from their rough coats.

"Look!" whispered Molly as the procession reached the platform and stopped in front of the King and Queen. "They're carrying something in their mouths."

Solemnly and one by one the donkeys approached the table and dropped something from their mouths. The King leaned over and looked curiously.

"They're oysters!" he said. He took a little knife from his pocket and prised one of them open.

"A pearl!" he cried. The crowd gasped and the King held up the pearl for them to see. It was twice the size of a pea and it gleamed softly in the sunlight.

Then the Mayor took out his penknife and opened the other five oysters, and, sure enough, each of them contained a large and beautiful pearl.

"What a splendid gift!" cried the Queen. "I shall wear the pearls in my crown. And we have seen the lucky sea horse after all!"

But the little sea horse was already on his way back to the sea. No one tried to stop him this time as he cantered lightly over the salty pebbles and on to the flat shining sands, golden hooves blinding in the sun. The waves seemed to run forward to meet him and with a last graceful leap he sprang into the waters of the bay and disappeared in a shower of spray.

The King and Queen were delighted and praised the Mayor for his common sense in dealing with the matter, so that when the parrot forgot his poem and got all the lines mixed up it didn't really matter at all.

The festival was declared open and the rest of the day was spent making merry. Garlands of flowers floated on the waters of the bay. The donkeys were none the worse for their adventures and ran up and down the sands giving rides till the sun went down.

Then at last the music stopped and the golden coach rolled away over the grey stone bridge into the mountains and the stars came out. Mr Winkle snored peacefully, still wearing his proud smile, and the parrot swinging in his cage out in the gusty porch suddenly remembered his poem and said it to the moon.

Over the bay the moon shone in a shining path. Crab in his hole, gull in his nest, shrimp in his pool, all were asleep. If Molly had not been asleep in the rocking *Tubby Boat* she might have seen a hundred sea horses leap from the waves and dance and frolic on the silvery sands.

And just before dawn the cold grey tide rushed up the sands in one vast smooth sweep and then ebbed as silently back again, washing away their hoof marks as it went. The sea keeps its secrets well.

A GIFT FROM WINKLESEA

Helen Cresswell

A trip to the seaside changes Dan and Mary's lives forever

The gift they bring back for their mother couldn't be more perfect – a beautiful bluish egg-shaped stone with gold lettering. They put it on the mantlepiece for everyone to admire.

And there it stays. Until Mary notices something strange about it – it feels warm to the touch – and sure enough, one day – it hatches . . .

ORDER FORM

☐ 0 340 63461 8   THE LITTLE SEA HORSE   £2.99
                     Helen Cresswell

☐ 0 340 10472 4   A GIFT FROM WINKLESEA   £8.99
                     Helen Cresswell (hardback)

☐ 0 340 64648 9   WHATEVER HAPPENED IN WINKLESEA   £8.99
                     Helen Cresswell (hardback)

☐ 0 340 64649 7   MYSTERY AT WINKLESEA   £8.99
                     Helen Cresswell (hardback)

☐ 0 340 61954 6   HAMISH   £2.99
                     W. J. Corbett

☐ 0 340 62653 4   PRINCE VINCE AND THE CASE OF   £2.99
                     THE SMELLY GOAT
                     Valerie Wilding

☐ 0 340 62654 2   PRINCE VINCE AND THE HOT DIGGORY DOG   £2.99
                     Valerie Wilding

All Hodder Children's books are available at your local bookshop or newsagent, or can be ordered direct from the publisher. Just tick the titles you want and fill in the form below. Prices and availability subject to change without notice.

Hodder Children's Books, Cash Sales Department, Bookpoint, 39 Milton Park, Abingdon, OXON, OX14 4TD, UK. If you have a credit card you may order by telephone – 01235 831700.

Please enclose a cheque or postal order made payable to Bookpoint Ltd to the value of the cover price and allow the following for postage and packing:
UK & BFPO: £1.00 for the first book, 50p for the second book and 30p for each additional book ordered up to a maximum charge of £3.00.
OVERSEAS & EIRE: £2.00 for the first book, £1.00 for the second book and 50p for each additional book.

Name...

Address ....

....

....

If you would prefer to pay by credit card, please complete:
Please debit my Visa / Access / Diner's Card / American Express (delete as applicable) card no:

Signature...

Expiry Date...